MW00583649

Lese is a writer from the upper west side of Manhattan

Ena is an illustrator from the Olympic city of Sarajevo. (enahodzic.com)

Charlotte's New York Adventure
A Girl With a Mission (June 2016)
A Meeting in Midtown (February 2018)

ISBN-13: 978-0692069240
duntonpublishing.com

Charlotte's
New York Adventure

A Meeting in Midtown

Lese Dunton

illustrations by Ena Hodzic

When we last left Charlotte she was ready with her plan.
All her buddies were on board and could understand.

The Statue will guide her, do you believe it?
With Liberty's wisdom, she knows she'll achieve it.

The team is assembled and ready to embark -
It does help to be friends with the Angel in the Park.

Hey Keith, let's go this way, to a really cool school.

Please tell me you're kidding. You think I'm a fool?

No no, you will like it, it's going to be fun.

We'll see how the changing of thinking is done.

The students playing instruments are trying to stay in tune.

Their music has no lyrics and they're going to need some soon.

Without the words on paper, how will the singers sing?

This writing is so stressful for a little girl named Ling.

Let's listen to her thoughts now -
to hear if they get shifted.
With help from the Green Lady,
I bet she'll be uplifted.

Ling:

Hey, what just happened?...It's amazing...all the words just seem to flow.

I understand so clearly, somehow everything I know.

My writing has great meaning that the music will enhance.

Each note from all the instruments makes every sentence dance!

Now that Ling is thinking right,
Let's head for a new start.
We'll show up at the theater
to find a change of heart.

Amber feels so sad and all alone, amidst the crowd.

She really wants to cry

when those around her laugh so loud.

How come no one loves her?

That is really how she's feeling.

I think it's time we bring in some Bethesda

Angel healing.

You can tell her heart has opened to the love that's truly there.

It comes from deep within her, sparked by Beth's angelic care.

Amber:

I'm feeling so much better, this is awesome, I am glowing.

Shakespeare sounds so beautiful.

Is there a second showing?

Inside me I am peaceful, full of wisdom, really good.

I even love this crowd of people in my neighborhood.

After all our efforts,

which were clearly quite successful,

we can hang out at the fountain

and then realize we are bless-full.

Whenever I have doubts again,
I hear my mother's tune,
it helps me to remember that my plans
will come true soon.

I'm still on all my missions, so it's not like I have fear...

I just need a different outlook,

so I'll see what we have here.

I should have told her she is worthy and creates such brilliant art...

but I must find New York Harbor, so the meeting can soon start.

This ocean is so wavy, it's a good thing I can swim,

I'm also glad I took those rowing classes at the gym.

Jennifer the Tugboat: The news has been confirmed,
they're coming soon, we know it's true.
The leaders of the world will meet,
deciding what to do.

Statue of Liberty: I've called two back-up angels,
one will stay at Empire State.
The other thinks the Chrysler's geometric shapes
are great.
They can float right into town within a lovely
rainbow bubble, but they better hurry up -
or else we could be in for trouble.

Keith: My iPad has the apps it needs, no problem,
I can carry it.

Angel Beth: The meeting starts tomorrow, in the
morning, at the Schmarriott.

Charlotte: Stay brave everybody,
I'm so glad we had this talk.
I'll see you all tomorrow,
Now I'm going for a walk.

Whenever my life starts to feel like a hassle,

I like to hide out up in Belvedere Castle.

By staring at the dark blue sky and all the stars
at night,

I know deep down within me that my life will work
out right.

These lovely little twinkly things are actually big
and bright,

They show me I can really turn the darkness
into light.

So now with these world leaders here, what is a girl to do?

Should I heal their hearts aplenty or just change their minds anew?

My team is waiting patiently to hear my great solution.

I may be onto something that will change our evolution.

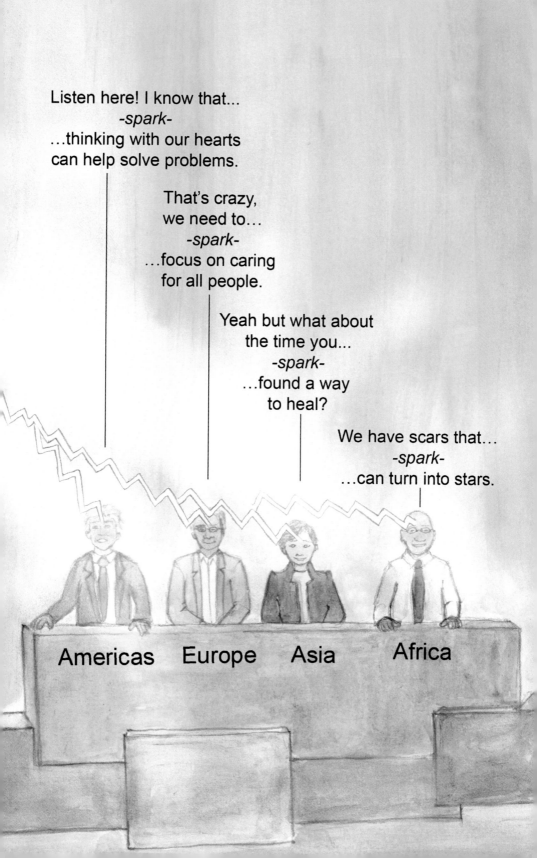

Good work, my friends, we did it!

Wasn't that so cool?

Let's all meet up later at our favorite fountain pool.

We'll have some more adventures soon - and not just midtown only.

We could go to Little Italy and eat a big cannoli!

We have a lot of friends these days no matter
where we go.

This joining heart and mind routine makes all
good fortunes grow.

You can look down at your feet you know,
or look straight up above -
the main thing to remember
is to focus on great love.

I have a question for you, if you'd like to take a chance.

I have this friend in Paris...would you like to visit France?

To be continued...

Made in the USA
Lexington, KY
11 March 2018